"I was born in London in 1946 and grew up in a sweet shop in Essex. For several years I worked as a graphic designer, but in 1980 I decided to concentrate on writing and illustrating books for children.

My wife, Annette, and I have two grown-up children, Ben and Amanda, and we have put down roots in Suffolk.

I haven't recently counted how many books there are with my name on the cover but Percy the Park Keeper accounts for a good many of them. I'm reliably informed that they have sold more than three million copies. Hooray!

I didn't realise this when I invented Percy, but I can now see that he's very like my mum's dad, my grandpa. I even have a picture of him giving a ride to my brother and me in his old home-made wooden wheelbarrow!"

NICK BUTTERWORTH

For Ringmaster and Mrs Naffs,
Captain Speedway and Uncle Lenny.
Most of all for Leon.

Everyone's Friend
PERCY

NICK BUTTERWORTH

HarperCollins *Children's Books*

Thanks Graham Daldry. You're a wizard.

Thanks Atholl McDonald. You're a hero!

First published in Great Britain by HarperCollins Publishers Ltd in 2001

ISBN-13: 978 0 00 778248 2
ISBN-10: 0 00 778248 9

Text and illustrations copyright © Nick Butterworth 2001
The author asserts the moral right to be identified as the author of the work.

Visit our website at: www.harpercollinschildrensbooks.co.uk

Printed and bound in Belgium

PERCY, THAT'S ME!

I'm Percy the Park Keeper. Looking after this beautiful park keeps me very busy. And then, on top of that, there always seems to be some little problem to sort out for a fox or a badger or a mole or a mouse. Still, I do like a bit of fun and mischief too.

I live in my cosy little hut by myself, but I'm never lonely. My friends, the animals, see to that. Aha! That sounds like someone at the door now. I'd better see who it is. Excuse me, won't you? If you head for the big oak tree by the lake, you're sure to bump into one or two of my friends on the way. I'll catch up with you and we can have a bit more of a chat. . .

Some people call this park Percy's Park, but it doesn't actually belong to me.

A long, long time ago, when some of the great oaks in the park were just acorns, someone built a magnificent house here. It had lovely gardens, a lake and a wonderful maze.

But one day, there was a fire and the great house burnt down. There are still some bits of it that you can see, but no one would want to live there now.

No, I prefer my old hut. It's quite big enough for me and there always seems to be room for my friends. Sometimes I think it must be bigger on the inside than it is on the outside. Perhaps it is!

I REALLY LIKE...

Spring time. I like the autumn too.
But especially the spring. And the autumn.

Stories. I like to read them, but I
enjoy listening to stories on the radio too.
And I enjoy telling them!

I DON'T LIKE . . .

Windy weather. It's exciting for clouds but
trees don't like it, and nor does my washing!

Being ill. But once in a while, I have
to let others take charge and I just have
to take my medicine.

I live on my own, so it's a mystery to me how I get through so much food.

I used to carry a heavy basketful of shopping back from the village shop every week. But one day, the handle of my basket broke and my shopping spilled all over the floor.

Mrs Purvis, the shopkeeper, came to my rescue (the owl thinks she likes me). She helped me to pick up my shopping. Then, she very generously gave me this old delivery bicycle. It makes shopping much easier. When I'm not using the bicycle for shopping, I can take all my friends for a spin around the park. Well, my animal friends, anyway. Perhaps not Mrs Purvis.

I've got lots of pictures in my photo album.

I tried to take a picture of myself with my camera on its automatic setting. I didn't see the molehill

A letter to Auntie Joyce. Hold tight badger! Don't post the mouse!

Here are just a few of me and some of my friends.

This is an old
picture of my
Great Uncle Jack
holding me.
Great Uncle Jack
was a fisherman.
I was a baby.

Guess
who!

If I'm not in my hut or out in the
park, you'll probably find me
in my workshop, fixing and
mending. I like to invent
things too.

Some of my inventions
work! Some don't.

My unsinkable boat sank. Luckily, the
mole is a good swimmer. My six-wheeled
barrow was quite good until I bumped over
a log. My five-wheeled barrow was not so
good. I usually get a lot of help when I'm
inventing but it's strange how some help
can actually make things take longer.

A PARK KEEPER'S DREAM

I'm always very busy,
  With lots to do and make.
I think it would be nice, sometimes,
  To have a little break . . .

Of course, I never work at night,
　Especially when I'm sleeping,
But once I had the strangest dream,
　A dream about park keeping!

First I had to comb the grass,
　And then to paint the hedges.
I chose a lovely shade of pink,
　(With purple round the edges).

I planted bulbs along the paths,
　And candles in the beds,
And they were lovely colours too,
　All blues and greens and reds.

All night I dug and raked and hoed,
　Inside the potting shed.
I worked so hard, when I got up,
　I went straight back to bed!

A FAVOURITE PLACE

Can you keep a secret? If you can, I'll tell you about a very special place in the park.

Follow the path by the stream up from the lake. You'll come to a place in the wood where the stream tumbles over a little waterfall. It's where I go when I want to sit and think.

It's a wonderful place to be when the sun is setting. But my favourite time is early in the morning. Mist floats over the pool and the little waterfall chatters away to itself as it sparkles in the early sunlight.

My friends know about this special place, but they usually don't disturb me. Once or twice, I have known a rabbit or a mouse to creep alongside me. Perhaps they wanted to do some thinking too.

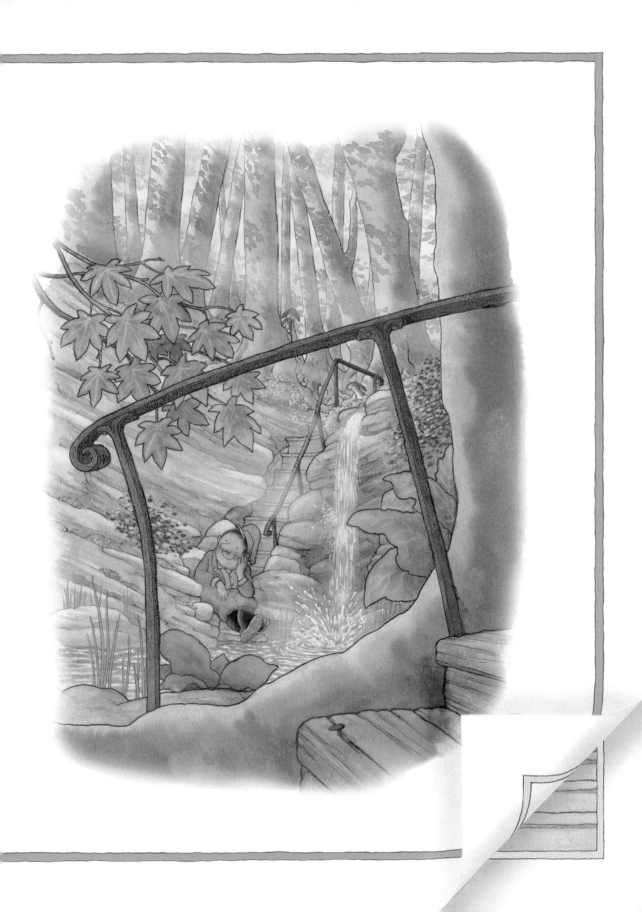

Here is another of my favourite places.
I like to visit my friends' tree house home
every day. I must have left that cheese
roll there yesterday. With the fox living
next door, I'm surprised it's still there!